The Waterslide

www.thewaterslide.com

Written by Brett A. Bodway   Illustrated by Dennis Krull

Contributions by Karen Duerre Bodway

Acknowledgments

I would like to take this opportunity to acknowledge the support I received from the following people who helped me in fulfilling Brett's dream of publishing this children's story:

• Tammy Noteboom for her recommendations, guidance, and great editing skills,

• Dennis Krull for his creative talents, formatting skills, and patience,

• Tania Thomas for her spiritual guidance,

• Roxane Beauclair Salonen for her suggestions and guidance,

• Catherine Graves for her suggestions and guidance,

• Brandon Conkins, for volunteering his time to the Big Brothers Big Sisters Program and being a great Big Brother to Grant,

• Susan Smith and the staff with the Big Brothers Big Sisters Program of The Village Family Service Center, Fargo, N.D.

• My friends and family.

Thank you all so much!

Karen Duerre Bodway

Dedication

This book is dedicated to the author and my late husband, Brett A. Bodway, who lost his life to complications from surgery to remove a brain tumor on March 17, 2010; seven days after his 47th birthday.

Brett was a wonderful father to our son, Grant, whom this book is also dedicated to as the main character of the story. Brett was a true family man and we miss him deeply.

Brett always wanted to make a difference. After his death, Grant was matched with a big brother from the Big Brothers Big Sisters Program of The Village Family Service Center in Fargo, N.D. Ten percent of the author proceeds from the sale of this book will be donated to this program to help make a difference.

One of Brett's dreams was to have a children's book published. This book is the result of me following through on his dream. I hope you enjoy the story.

Karen Duerre Bodway

"Alright campers, listen up!"

Coach Johnson barked out the instructions above the chattering to get everyone's attention. "As many of you boys know, this year we'll have a camp Olympics, complete with individual medals and team trophies."

The boys responded with cheers and high-five slapping. Everyone except Grant, who wanted to run and hide.

He was starting to feel depressed about the announcement and wanted to be someplace else.

"The events will take place tomorrow, so I want you to pick teams of four members right now."
Coach Johnson added.

"The team with the most points will

win the camp Olympics.

Individuals will be awarded four points

for a first-place gold medal,

three points for second-place silver, and

two points for third-place bronze.

I have chosen captains for each team.

Ryan is captain of the Blue Team, Jake for

the Red Team, Kyle for the Green Team,

and Bart for the Orange Team."

Grant's stomach churned.

They're always the captains, he thought.

This will be just like at school,

I'll be picked last again, and then

my whole summer at camp will be ruined.

The captains started picking teams; the older boys were picked first. Grant was only eleven, but he knew why he would be picked last. Not because of his age, but because he wasn't good at sports. He never could play as well as the other boys; he was smaller, skinnier, and weaker. He was dreading the moment when no one else was left to pick except him.

It made him uncomfortable to go to the team that had to take him. As the group dwindled, he once again found himself alone.

All eyes were on him,

as the coach shouted out,

"And Grant fills out

the Green Team."

Grant walked to the group of boys with his head down and listened to their groans of disappointment as they realized he was on their team.

"OK, listen up!" Coach Johnson barked again after the teams were chosen. "The four events this year are the 100-yard dash, the javelin throw, the long jump, and the waterslide. Each team member will compete in one event only, so everyone will have a chance to participate, and it will truly be a team effort."

The teams huddled together to start planning their strategy. Grant gathered in with his Green Team.

"OK, who will run the 100?" asked Kyle, the captain.

"Tony is fast! He should do it," Phil said.

"Yeah, Tony!" the rest of the team agreed.

"Phil, you have the best arm, so you should do the javelin throw, and I can jump the farthest, so that leaves the waterslide for you, Grant," Kyle said.

The dinner bell rang and the boys scattered as they ran to the mess hall.

Grant stood motionless.

He hung his head and pondered how he could avoid the embarrassment of having to participate and letting his teammates down.

After dinner, Grant went to the recreation center to telephone his dad.

"Hi, Dad, can you come get me?"

His voice trembled.

"What's wrong, son?" his dad asked.

"Nobody likes me here, and I have to go down the waterslide tomorrow."

"Oh, I'm sure they'll like you once they get to know you."

"They won't when they see I can't go down the waterslide," Grant said.

it's 19 steps high!

That's higher than your ladder!"

Grant's voice squeaked at the thought of such a height. He had climbed that ladder to the roof of the house last summer, and when he reached the top he looked down to see how high it was. That's when he became scared of heights. Now he was afraid to climb anything.

"Well, maybe I can help you," replied Dad.
"You weren't afraid of heights before you
climbed the ladder, right?"

"No," Grant admitted.

"Well, that just proves that the fear is
all in your mind. So all you have to do is think
of something else, and the fear should disappear.
When you climb those steps think that you're
climbing the steps to the kitchen in the house.

You're not afraid of that, are you?" Dad said.

"No," said Grant.

"And when you get to the top and lie down to slide, keep your eyes closed and think about lying down on the Slip n' Slide in the backyard. Stretch your arms out in front of you and slide down while you think about sliding on the lawn with your friends. If you think about those things, you'll be able to do it. OK?" Dad said.

"I guess." Grant was not really convinced.

"It's like dreaming.

If you pretend that you're actually doing

those things, it will seem like you're there

in your mind," added his dad.

Grant walked back to his bunk,

trying to imagine how this would work for

tomorrow's big test. He decided he would go

to sleep and try to dream about the

Slip n' Slide in his backyard.

1ST BLUE
2ND GREEN
3RD RED
4TH ORANGE

The next day Grant watched as his teammates competed in three events.

The Green Team was just three points out of first, and the waterslide was the last event.

The Blue Team had just finished up.
Grant would be next. A first-place finish would give them the points needed to win the Olympics, and Grant a gold medal to show his dad.

The object of the waterslide competition was to be the fastest down the slide and then swim underwater to the finish line.

Two of the boys came up for air before crossing the finish line, and the leading Blue Team did it in 12.8 seconds.

Grant approached the stairs to the waterslide.

He remembered what his dad had told him,
and thought about his mom calling him upstairs
for dinner. In his mind he climbed each stair to
the kitchen in slow motion.

When he reached the top, he opened his eyes.

He was so high up!

He quickly lay down and grabbed the sides
of the slide. He heard his teammates cheering
him on, unaware that he was frozen by fear.

Grant desperately searched his mind.

The cheering turned to playful chatter as he imagined all of them in his backyard.

They were playing with the Slip n' Slide and having a good time.
At the same time, he relaxed.

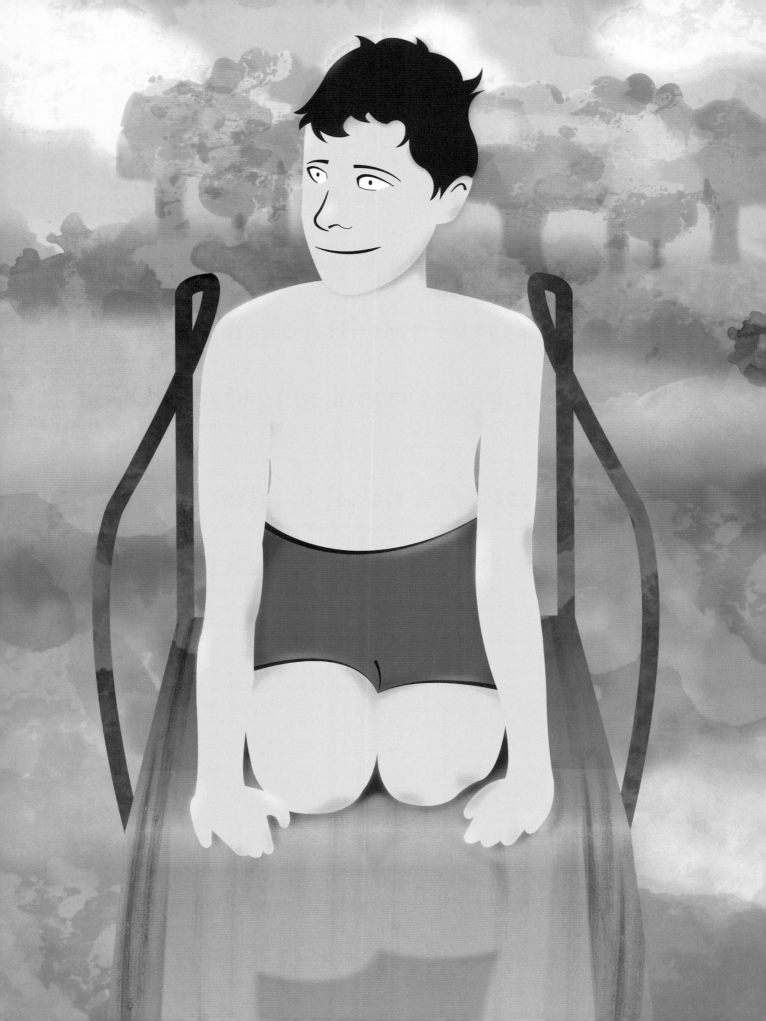

He stretched his arms in front of him and began the journey down the slide. He gained speed the farther down he went until the water hit his hands. He jettisoned through the water like a torpedo as he kicked toward the finish line.

Grant surfaced for air as his teammates cheered. "10.6 seconds!" shouted Coach Johnson.

"You did it!"

Kyle yelled, as he pulled Grant from the water.

"We won the Olympics!" Phil shouted.

Tony handed the first place trophy to Grant.

Then the team hoisted him on their shoulders.

They paraded around the campground for
all to see who the champion was.

Grant knew he would never be
picked last again.

What do you do to
help overcome your fears?

Making A Difference

Big Brothers Big Sisters
of The Village Family Service Center

We are here to Start Something.

Big Brothers Big Sisters is not your typical organization. We help children realize their potential and build their futures. We nurture children and strengthen communities.

Changing perspectives. Changing lives.

For more than 100 years, Big Brothers Big Sisters has operated under the belief that inherent in every child is the ability to succeed and thrive in life. As the nation's largest donor and volunteer supported mentoring network, Big Brothers Big Sisters makes meaningful, monitored matches between adult volunteers ("Bigs") and children ("Littles"), ages 6 through 18, in communities across the country. We develop positive relationships that have a direct and lasting effect on the lives of young people. In the Fargo-Moorhead area, BBBS has been a program of The Village Family Service Center since 1973. School based mentoring was added in 1998.

Our Programs Start Something

Here's the proof. National research has shown that positive relationships between Littles and their Bigs have a direct and measurable impact on children's lives. By participating in our programs,

Little Brothers and Sisters are:

- More confident in their schoolwork performance
- Able to get along better with their families
- 46% less likely to begin using illegal drugs
- 27% less likely to begin using alcohol
- 52% less likely to skip school.

Volunteer or donate to BBBS and you could be the start of something big!

Grant and Brandon, matched 9/30/10

What can you do to make a difference?

Autographs

Kendall,

Cameron,

Always do your best!

Karen Duerre Bodway

Grant
Bodway

The Waterslide

www.thewaterslide.com

Made in the USA
Charleston, SC
27 August 2012